YOGA ANIMALS IN THE FOREST

CHRISTIANE KERR

ILLUSTRATED BY JULIA GREEN

Kane Miller
A DIVISION OF EDC PUBLISHING

ABOUT THIS BOOK

In this book, you will read about Bear's journey through the forest.

Along the way, Bear will meet friends who will teach her how to do some simple yoga poses.

First, Bear will learn why each pose is helpful, and you'll see her try them out.

Then, it's your turn.

Look at the panel at the bottom of each page, like the example below. Don't worry if you don't get it right the first time—keep practicing and have fun!

Look at the panel at the bottom of the page.

Read the instructions to follow the pose.

CAN YOU DO IT, TOO?

1. Stand up straight. Bring the palms of your hands together by your heart.

2. With one foot on the ground, place your other foot on the inside of your standing leg, just below your knee.

3. Raise your hands above your head. Think happy thoughts, and smile!

4. Try to balance for three breaths. Repeat with your other leg.

The yoga exercises in this book should be practiced with the help of an adult. It is recommended that children attempt the poses on a yoga mat. For the full benefits of each pose, see pages 30–31.

Bear woke up from a long, deep sleep.
She yawned a great big

Y-A-W-N,

and tried hard to keep
her eyes open.

"I do this when I
want to wake up,"
said Rabbit.

Bear stood very still and breathed, just like Rabbit. And Bear started to feel more awake.

CAN YOU DO IT, TOO?

1. Stand with your feet slightly apart, arms by your sides.

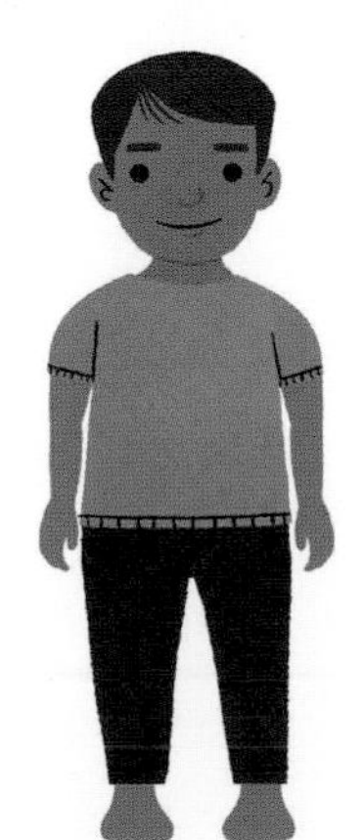

2. Take a big bear breath:

- a long breath in through your nose;
- a breath out through your mouth.

3. Repeat this two more times.

After such a long sleep, Bear felt a little grouchy.

"I balance myself like this," said Bird.

Bear stood on one leg, and then on the other, just like Bird. And a smile spread across Bear's face.

CAN YOU DO IT, TOO?

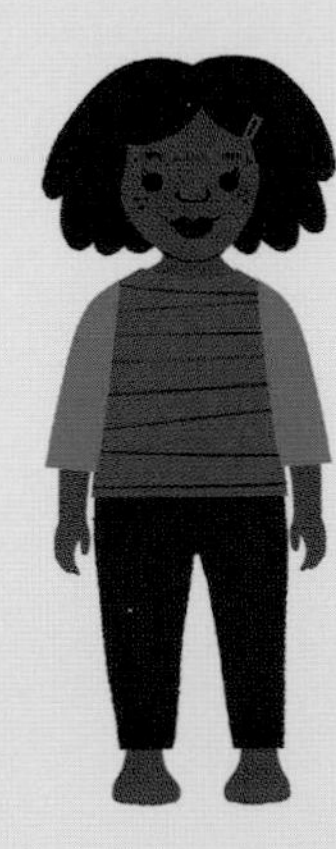

1. Stand up straight. Bring the palms of your hands together by your heart.

2. With one foot on the ground, place your other foot on the inside of your standing leg, just below your knee.

3. Raise your hands above your head. Think happy thoughts, and smile!

4. Try to balance for three breaths. Repeat with your other leg.

All Bear wanted
now was to
have a good long
S-T-R-E-T-C-H.

"Sometimes, I
reach up and try
to touch the sky!"
said Chipmunk.

Bear stretched
and stretched,
just like Chipmunk.
And Bear thought
how wonderful
it was to live
in the forest.

CAN YOU DO IT, TOO?

1. Standing up straight, breathe in, and lift your arms above your head. Stretch your fingertips up to the sky.

2. Breathe out, and stretch to one side. Breathe in as you go back to standing up straight. Stretch to the other side as you breathe out.

3. Repeat once more on each side.

Walking through the trees,
Bear wondered what to do next.

"Every morning, I try to think clearly
about the day ahead," said Mouse.

Bear pressed her paws together at her knees, and closed her eyes, just like Mouse. And a clear thought appeared in Bear's head.

CAN YOU DO IT, TOO?

1. Stand up straight with your feet hip-distance apart.

2. Bend your knees and go down into a squat. With your knees and big toes pointed out, balance on the balls of your feet. Rest your elbows on your knees and bring the tips of your fingers and thumbs together.

3. Breathe in and, as you breathe out, say quietly, "Concentration is my strength."

"If I follow
Bee," said Bear,
"I might find my
favorite food."

"I sniff for my food
like this," said Fox.

Bear dropped to the ground and sniffed, just like Fox. And Bear could smell all the wonderful smells of the forest.

CAN YOU DO IT, TOO?

1. Kneel with your hands flat on the ground.

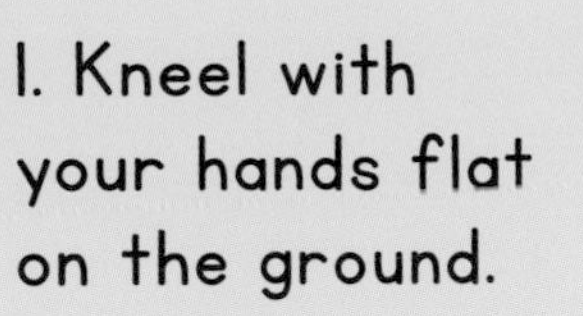

2. Curl your toes under, lift your hips and bottom, and gently straighten your legs.

3. Start slowly walking around. Walk your right hand and left foot forward at the same time.

4. Do the same with your left hand and right foot. Notice what you can see, hear, and smell.

Bear rushed quickly
from tree to tree, but
didn't find any food.

"I try to wait and
listen for my food,"
said Weasel.

Bear waited and listened, just like Weasel. And Bear could hear all the beautiful sounds of the forest.

CAN YOU DO IT, TOO?

1. Kneel with your hands and knees on the ground, and your back straight. Stretch out your hands and fingers, noticing where you touch the ground.

2. Breathe in as you bring your shoulder blades together, dropping your tummy toward the ground. Look ahead, and smile!

3. Breathe out and arch your back up toward the sky, letting the top of your head drop toward the ground. Breathe in, and come back to the starting pose.

Bear thought she saw some food up in the branches. But then she heard a loud

H-I-S-S!

"When I want to warn bears to leave me alone, I do this," said Snake.

Bear lay down flat and hissed, just like Snake. And Bear remembered that she should take care in the forest.

CAN YOU DO IT, TOO?

1. Lie flat on the ground with your hands underneath your shoulders, palms down, and fingertips pointing forward. Keep your elbows close to your body.

2. Breathe in and, as you breathe out, try to stretch your back as you slowly lift your head and chest off the ground. Keep your tummy on the ground, and look straight ahead, relaxing your shoulders.

3. Take three quiet breaths here, making a hissing sound as you breathe out.

At last, Bear found a beehive. It was full of honey, but surrounded by bees.

"I stay still this way," said Butterfly, "so that I don't get stung."

Bear stayed very still, just like Butterfly. And Bear could hear the bees and smell the flowers.

CAN YOU DO IT, TOO?

1. Kneel with your hands and knees on the ground, with your knees and feet together.

2. Slowly sit back on your heels and rest your hands on your legs, palms facing down.

3. Sit still here—can you feel your breath moving in your body?

Bear dipped her paw, and ate
some of the delicious honey.

"Can you show me how you
make your buzzing noise?"
Bear asked Bee.

"I use my wings,"
said Bee, "but you
can use your lips."

Bear sat and breathed, and buzzed, just like Bee. And Bear felt as if she was not just full of honey, but full of bees, too!

Buzzzzzzzzzzz

Buzzzzzzzzzz

CAN YOU DO IT, TOO?

1. Sit with your legs wide apart, then bend one leg in toward yourself. Bring the other leg in front to sit in a simple cross-legged pose. Rest your hands on your knees.

2. Sit with your back straight. With your lips together and your teeth slightly apart, make a gentle buzzing sound as you breathe out. Repeat this three times, noticing what the buzz feels like inside your body.

Bear rested by
the river for a
while, happy to have
eaten her fill.

“I do this when I feel
grateful,” said Frog.

Bear sat down and touched her toes, just like Frog. And Bear thought about what a wonderful day it had been.

CAN YOU DO IT, TOO?

1. Sit with your legs straight out in front of you, bending your knees slightly if you need to. Settle your bottom on the ground as you sit up straight. Rest your hands on your legs.

2. Breathe in and, as you breathe out, slide your hands down your legs toward your feet, bringing your head down and keeping your back as straight as you can. Breathe in and, as you breathe out, rest.

It was getting dark, and Bear started to worry about finding her way back home.

"Everyone gets worried sometimes, however big or small they are," said Mole. "I do this to keep calm."

Bear rested her head and breathed, just like Mole. And all the worries in Bear's head floated away.

CAN YOU DO IT, TOO?

1. Start by kneeling with your bottom on your heels and your knees a little apart.

2. Use your hands to support you as you lower your forehead, gently resting it on the ground. Bring your arms alongside your body, with your palms facing up. Take four quiet breaths.

When Bear got home
to her cave, she sat and
watched the sun go down.

For a moment, Bear felt lonely.
Then she gave herself a big bear hug, and made a list in her head of all the things the other animals had shared with her.

CAN YOU DO IT, TOO?

1. Lie on your back, with your feet flat on the floor and your knees pointing up toward the sky, your arms by your sides, and your palms facing up.

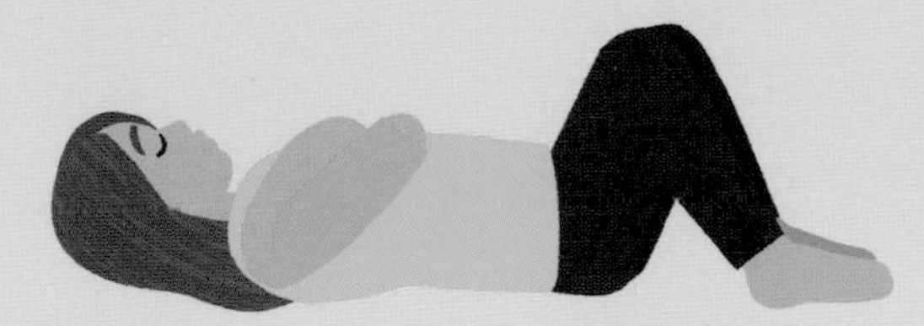

2. Breathe in, bringing your arms across your body and your hands beneath your shoulders to give yourself a big hug. Breathe out and rest.

3. As you breathe, make these three wishes for yourself: "May I be happy. May I be well. May I be calm." Cross your arms the other way and repeat the three wishes.

Bear had learned to wake up like Rabbit, balance like Bird, stretch like Chipmunk, think clearly like Mouse, sniff like Fox, listen like Weasel, hiss like Snake, stay still like Butterfly, buzz like Bee, feel grateful like Frog, and keep calm like Mole.

CAN YOU DO IT, TOO?

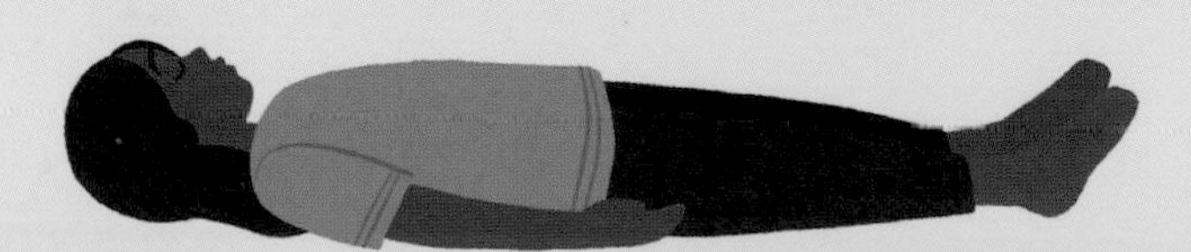

1. Lie on the ground with your legs straight, your arms by your sides, and your palms facing up.

But now all she wanted to do was ...

... sleep like Bear.

2. Breathe in and, as you breathe out, rest into the ground. Let your body feel soft and relaxed.

3. Notice where you feel your breath moving in your body. Maybe you can feel it in your tummy, your chest, or your nose? Lie here as long as you like, and pay attention to your breath and body.

POSE BENEFITS

WAKE UP LIKE RABBIT

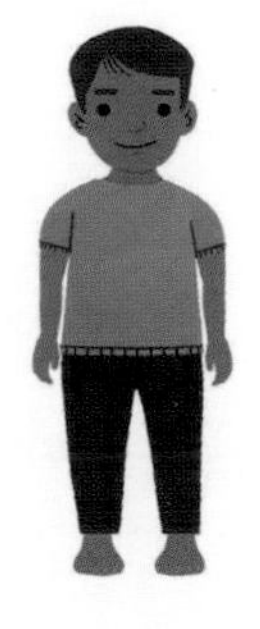

- Promotes calm
- Centers the body
- Encourages good posture
- Improves steadiness
- Can do it anywhere

BALANCE LIKE BIRD

- Increases focus and concentration
- Improves balance
- Strengthens
- Builds confidence and happiness

STRETCH LIKE CHIPMUNK

- Warms up the body
- Rejuvenates
- Stretches the spine in all directions
- Promotes calm
- Helps digestion

THINK CLEARLY LIKE MOUSE

- Increases focus and concentration
- Stretches the hips and back
- Strengthens
- Improves balance
- Helps digestion

SNIFF LIKE FOX

- Stretches the back, neck, legs, and arms
- Strengthens the shoulders and arms
- Improves balance
- Develops body awareness

LISTEN LIKE WEASEL

- Stretches the front and back of the spine
- Develops breath and body awareness
- Strengthens and stretches the wrists

HISS LIKE SNAKE

- Energizes
- Strengthens the spine
- Stretches the front of the body
- Develops breath awareness

STAY STILL LIKE BUTTERFLY

- Promotes calm
- Helps with grounding
- Stretches the thighs

BUZZ LIKE BEE

- Promotes calm
- Increases focus and concentration
- Develops body awareness

FEEL GRATEFUL LIKE FROG

- Promotes calm
- Stretches the back of the body, including the legs
- Improves circulation
- Increases focus and concentration

KEEP CALM LIKE MOLE

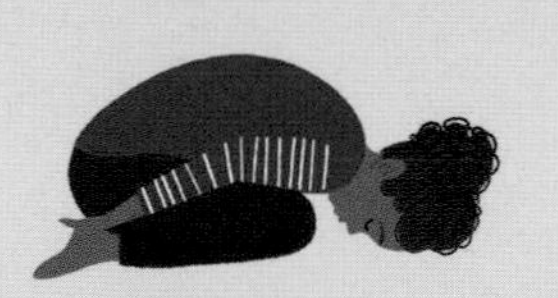

- Promotes calm
- Relieves stress
- Stretches the back
- Improves sleep

REMEMBER LIKE BEAR

- Promotes calm
- Encourages self-soothing
- Stretches the shoulders

SLEEP LIKE BEAR

- Promotes calm
- Develops breath and body awareness
- Restores mind and body
- Increases relaxation

First American Edition 2020
Kane Miller, A Division of EDC Publishing

For information contact:
Kane Miller, A Division of EDC Publishing
PO Box 470663
Tulsa, OK 74147-0663
www.kanemiller.com
www.edcpub.com
www.usbornebooksandmore.com

Library of Congress Control Number: 2019952400

Manufactured in Guangdong, China TT072020

ISBN: 978-1-68464-087-4

2 3 4 5 6 7 8 9 10